The Berenstain Bears
GO TO THE DOCTOR

Take a deep breath.
Stick out your tongue.
Come see Doctor Grizzly
While you are young.

A FIRST TIME BOOK®

The Berenstain Bears
GO TO THE DOCTOR

Stan & Jan Berenstain

Random House New York

Copyright © 1981 by Berenstain Enterprises, Inc. All rights reserved. Published in the United States by Random House
Children's Books, a division of Random House, Inc., New York. Random House and the colophon are registered trademarks
of Random House, Inc. First Time Books and the colophon are registered trademarks of Berenstain Enterprises, Inc.
randomhouse.com/kids   BerenstainBears.com
Library of Congress Cataloging-in-Publication Data
Berenstain, Stan. The Berenstain bears go to the doctor. (Berenstain bears first time books)
Summary: Dr. Grizzly gives the Berenstain cubs a regular checkup.
ISBN 978-0-394-84835-8 (trade) — ISBN 978-0-375-98254-5 (ebook)
[1. Medical care—Fiction. 2. Bears—Fiction.] I. Berenstain, Jan. II. Title. PZ7.B4483Ber [E] AACR2 81-50043
Printed in the United States of America 100 99 98 97 96 95 94 93 92 91 90

"Tomorrow," said Mama Bear as she helped the cubs get ready for bed, "you'll be going to the doctor for a checkup."

"Doctor?" said Brother Bear. "We're not sick!"

"And what's a checkup?" asked Sister Bear, a little worried.

"It's just what it sounds like," said Mama. "Dr. Grizzly will check to see if you are growing the way healthy cubs should."

"Will it hurt?"
asked Sister, pulling
the covers up close.

"Now, now," said Papa Bear as he kissed her good night. "You just settle down. There's absolutely nothing to worry about."

But Sister wasn't so sure.

The next morning, after a good breakfast, the family got into their red roadster and were on their way.

"Do you ever get checkups, Mama?"
Sister asked as they drove along the
dusty dirt road.

"Yes, I do," answered Mama.

"*I* don't need checkups anymore," bragged Papa. "Because I . . . I . . .

AH-CHOO

never get sick."

"That was quite a sneeze," said Mama.

"It's this dusty road," said Papa, turning onto the main highway into Beartown.

They pulled to a stop in front of the doctor's office.

"Come, cubs!" said Mama. "We don't want to be late for our appointment."

But Brother held back. He remembered something.

"Are we going to get shots?" he asked.

"That's up to . . . to . . . to . . .

-AH CHOO!

. . . the doctor," said Papa, sneezing an even bigger sneeze than before.

"Bless you!" said Mama.

"It's just this bright sunlight," sniffed Papa. "I *never* get sick."

The doctor's waiting room was a busy,
cheerful place with pictures on the
walls, books to look at, and puzzles
to do. Brother started a puzzle. Sister
took a book, but didn't really look at
it. Other bears were coming in—and she
looked around the room at them. There
were cubs of all ages with their parents.

Some of the smallest cubs looked a little worried.
Sister smiled at them so they wouldn't be afraid.

There was a big
cub with a cast on
his leg. It had
names and funny
drawings all over
it.

He let Brother
write his name
on it for luck,
and Sister drew
a picture.

There was even a little baby cub only a few weeks old.

"Next!" called Dr. Grizzly. It was Brother's and Sister's turn.

Dr. Grizzly was friendly, but she got right down to work. She had a lot of bears to take care of and not much time to waste.

First, she weighed and measured the cubs.

"Fine!" she said. "You've both gained weight nicely, and grown taller."

She listened to their chests with a stethoscope.

And poked them all over to check on everything inside.

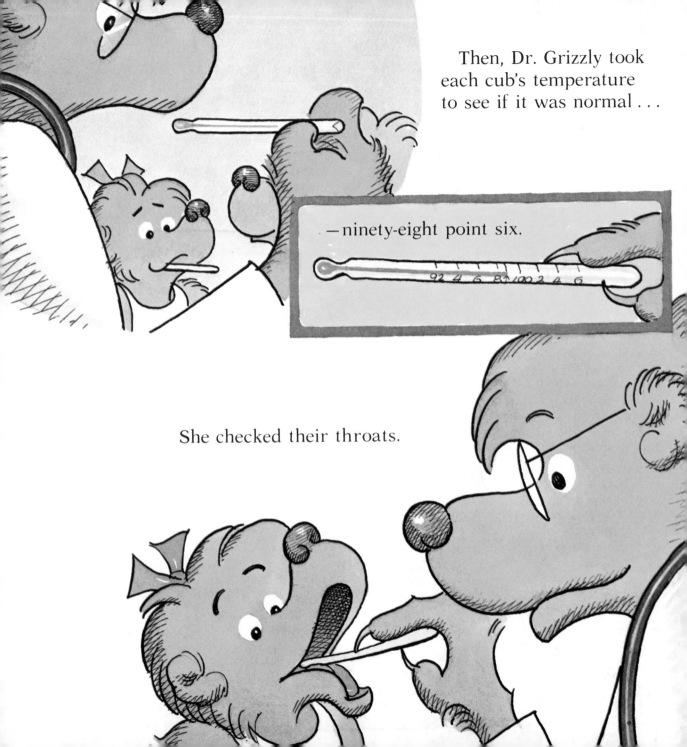

Then, Dr. Grizzly took each cub's temperature to see if it was normal . . .

—ninety-eight point six.

She checked their throats.

Then, she looked at their eyes,

ears,

and noses with a
special little light.

Next, she tested their hearing
by whispering very softly.

Then came the eye test. Brother read every letter except the very smallest. Sister didn't know all the letters yet, so she read a special chart that looked like this:

"Very good!" said the doctor, as she studied some papers in a folder.

Sister whispered to Brother, "So far, it hasn't hurt at all!"

"Well, that pretty much takes care of it," said
Dr. Grizzly, looking through her eyeglasses
at the papers, "except for one thing. I see it's time for
your booster shots."

"I knew it!" said Brother.

"Why do we have to have shots when we're not even
sick?" said Sister.

"Now, Sister," said Papa, "the doc . . . doc . . . doc . . .
AH-CHOO! . . . doctor knows best!"

"Bless you," said Dr. Grizzly. "And that's a very
good question, Sister. . . . "

As she got the shots ready, she called out into the
waiting room, "I've got a brave little cub in here who's
going to show you all how to take a shot!"

"Getting back to your question, Sister," said Dr. Grizzly. "You see, there are some kinds of medicine that you take after you get sick, and those are very useful. But this kind of shot is a special medicine that keeps you from *getting* sick."

"Will it hurt?" asked Sister.

"Not nearly as much as biting your tongue or bumping your shin," the doctor explained. "There! All done!"

Dr. Grizzly was right! And it happened so fast that Sister didn't even have time to say ouch!

The little cubs who were watching were *very* impressed.

So was Brother.

After Brother's shot, Papa said, "Well, Doctor, we'll be go . . . go . . . go . . .

CHOO!

—going now."

"Just a minute, Papa Bear," said Dr. Grizzly.
"Let me have a look at you."
"But, I *never* get sick. . . ." Papa started to say.

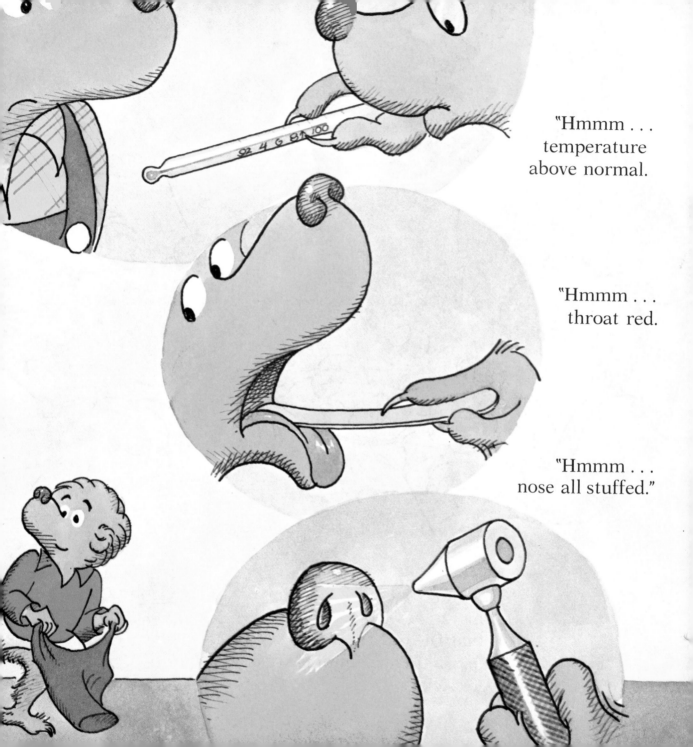

"Hmmm . . .
temperature
above normal.

"Hmmm . . .
throat red.

"Hmmm . . .
nose all stuffed."

"Time for your medicine, Papa!" said the cubs, offering him a big spoonful of the gooey pink stuff that Dr. Grizzly prescribed for his cold.

"Well," said Papa, smiling weakly, "I *hardly* ever get sick!"